This book belongs to:

_____

_____

_____

To Lili and her daily stack of books
To Fabienne, Michel, and Cyril

Little Unicorn is SCARED

Aurélie Chien Chow Chine

LITTLE, BROWN AND COMPANY

NEW YORK   BOSTON

This is Little Unicorn.
He is very much like all the other little unicorns....

Sometimes, **Little Unicorn** is happy.
Sometimes, he is **not** happy.
Sometimes, he is sad.
Sometimes, he is scared.
Sometimes, he is angry.

These are emotions.

And **Little Unicorn** feels all kinds of emotions.
Just like you.

But there is something that makes **Little Unicorn** special:
He has a **magical mane**!

When all is well, his mane shines
with the colors of the rainbow.

But when all isn't well, his mane changes...
and its color shows just what he feels.

Happy

Jealous

Angry

Guilty

Shy

Scared

Stubborn

Sad

How does **Little Unicorn** feel today?

Awful!

His heart feels dark and stormy,
and he's going to tell us why.

And you, how do you feel today?

Great

Good

Fine

Not good

Bad

Awful

Now, why does **Little Unicorn** feel bad?

During the day, he is happy and full of life!

Little Unicorn loves playing outside and spending his time looking at trees, flowers, and butterflies.

But at night, everything gets very dark.

Little Unicorn feels a little worried.
He doesn't really like it when night comes
because he knows he'll have to
go to bed soon.

Little Unicorn is full of ideas of how to delay bedtime.

During dinner, he eats his peas one by one.

When it's time for a bedtime story, he collects a big stack of books. Maybe Mama will read them all?

Little Unicorn even finds some great hiding places!

But nothing works.
It's late....He must go to bed.

Little Unicorn has to fall asleep in the dark.
He's scared.

As if nighttime wasn't dark enough,
he has to close his eyes!

Mama and Papa comfort him. They remind him
that they will be in the room next door.

But as soon as **Little Unicorn** is alone
in his room, he is really scared.

Little Unicorn shivers.

What if he had an armor of courage to tame his fear?

He does! He has his breath.

When you feel scared, you can do this
breathing exercise to give you courage, too.

Breathing exercise to tame your fear

1 **Little Unicorn** closes his eyes.
He breathes in through his nose and holds his breath.
Then he puts both his hands on his head.
He imagines strong armor that will protect him.

2 **Little Unicorn** keeps holding his breath and draws his armor of courage in the air with his hands: He draws it from the top of his head down to his feet.

3 Protected by his armor,
Little Unicorn blows all his breath out hard.
He tames his fear!

4 **Little Unicorn** does this
exercise **three times**.
It takes at least **three breaths**
to make his armor as bright as the sun.

Then **Little Unicorn** takes a normal breath.
He is no longer afraid of the dark, and he sleeps peacefully,
with all kinds of amazing dreams about
wearing his golden armor.

In the morning, **Little Unicorn** wakes up in great shape!

His good mood is back,
and the rainbow has returned to his mane.

If you tame your fear with an armor of courage,
you will feel relieved, too.
And your **smile** will return!

Don't miss these other stories about Little Unicorn!

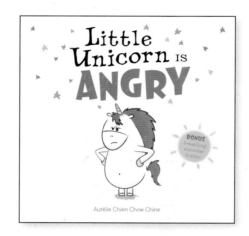

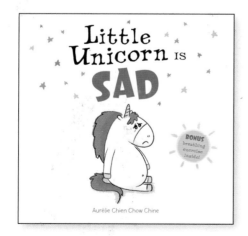

Coming soon!

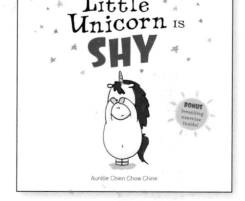

Coming soon!